ONYEKA

I am a reader and I celebrated

WORLD BOOK DAY 2024

with this gift from my local bookseller
and Simon & Schuster Children's Books.

....

**READ ALL OF THE BOOKS IN
THE ONYEKA SERIES!**

ONYEKA
AND THE ACADEMY
OF THE SUN

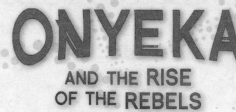

ONYEKA
AND THE RISE
OF THE REBELS

ONYEKA
AND THE HEROES
OF THE DAWN

ONYEKA

AND THE SECRET SUPERHERO

Tọlá Okogwu

SIMON & SCHUSTER

First published in Great Britain in 2024 by Simon & Schuster UK Ltd

1 3 5 7 9 10 8 6 4 2

Simon & Schuster UK Ltd
1st Floor, 222 Gray's Inn Road
London WC1X 8HB

www.simonandschuster.co.uk
www.simonandschuster.com.au
www.simonandschuster.co.in

Simon & Schuster Australia, Sydney
Simon & Schuster India, New Delhi

A CIP catalogue record for this book
is available from the British Library.

PB ISBN 978-1-3985-2869-7
eBook ISBN 978-1-3985-2871-0
eAudio ISBN 978-1-3985-2870-3

Typeset in Garamond by M Rules
Printed and Bound using 100% Renewable
Electricity at CPI Group (UK) Ltd

WORLD BOOK DAY ®

World Book Day's mission is to offer every
child and young person the opportunity to
read and love books by giving you the
chance to have a book of your own.

To find out more, and for fun activities including
video stories, audiobooks and book recommendations,
visit worldbookday.com

World Book Day is a charity sponsored by
National Book Tokens.

CHAPTER
ONE

Sand is lodged in my telekinetic hair! A long, thick, coily strand the shade of midnight drifts across my face, blocking my view of the crystal-clear sea stretching out before me. Its foamy waves lap against the soft white sand that cushions my feet, while the sun warms my skin. I can feel its heat even with the tall palm trees looming above me. Their vibrant green fronds sway in the gentle breeze as they curve protectively round the coconuts clustered beneath them. Using Ike, my special superpower, I pull the loose strand of hair back up into the bun on top of my head just by thinking about it. A loud whoop comes from somewhere in the water and I turn in the direction of the noise.

Ibeno Beach in Nigeria is the longest sand beach in West Africa, but today it's deserted except for the four of us. I spy my friends Hassan and Niyì immediately. Both dressed in swimming trunks, Niyì, the taller and broader of the two, reaches towards Hassan to try to dunk him in the calm Atlantic Ocean. Hassan slips away easily, his onyx-coloured skin gleaming like a polished pebble.

Suddenly, Niyì's hand darts out and an icy blast shoots from it, solidifying on top of the water in a long oval shape. He climbs on quickly and balances on his very own surfboard of superpowered ice, which isn't easily melted or broken. Niyì is a cryo-emitter. He's also a bit of a show-off.

Not to be beaten, Hassan lifts his hand and a yellow bubble of energy forms round him instantly. His Ike is energy emission, and he usually uses his energy fields to turn invisible and avoid trouble. Not today though. Instead, he levitates above the water and a triumphant grin blooms on his face as he manoeuvres the energy field around Niyì in a strange game of water tag. Another shout of joy from Hassan has me itching to join them. My swimming skills have improved in the seven months since my powers first surfaced when I saved my best friend, Cheyenne, in a pool back in London.

A quick glance at the girl beside me tells me it's probably not a good idea to follow the boys into the water. Light brown legs peek out from a pair of yellow shorts, the outfit completed by a matching top. Adanna's even lighter brown locs are pulled into a high bun, and her hawk-eyed attention is fixed on the green-and-white device resting in the sand in front of her. It looks like a giant boomerang, except it has four robotic legs and solar panels cover its surface. Adanna's busy hands tinker with a tangle of multicoloured wires spilling out of an open panel in the side of the device. The look of concentration on her face would better suit an adult, not the teenage girl before me.

We're all the same age, but Adanna's a genius, so everything she does and says *feels* old. Above her, a drone hovers, its blades whirring as it keeps a protective watch over its creator. Adanna is a technopath *and* a synaesthetic empath, which basically means she can control technology as well as sense emotions. It makes being her friend *very* interesting.

'I know we're here to work, but you could try relaxing for once,' I finally say with a sigh.

'I am relaxed.' Adanna's fingers don't stop moving, her face twisted in thought. 'You do remember we're not actually at Ibeno Beach, right?' Her hand lifts, waving towards our beautiful surroundings. 'No matter how real this all looks.'

She's right, as usual. Everything around us, from the bright blue water to the pale sand, is a holographic projection. It looks, feels and smells so real, though, that for a brief moment I'd forgotten we were still at the Academy of the Sun, a special school for genetically enhanced children like us – or Solari, as we're otherwise known. We're in the Holographic Offensive Multisensory Environment, to be precise, or HOME. It's where we learn how to harness our special superpower that's categorized in one of four ways – Psionics, Emitters, Transformers and Enhancers.

Seven months ago, I was a regular kid living in London with my mum. Okay, maybe not regular, because of how big my hair is. Reaching almost to my bum, the thick mass of tight coils is currently styled in

4

braided bantu knots. But my life changed completely when my mum dropped the bomb that I was a Psionic Solari. We returned to Nigeria, the technologically advanced country where my parents are from, and went to the Academy of the Sun. Since then, I've discovered my long-lost father and an aunt, who are both Solari. I also helped save the academy from its evil former head teacher, Dr Dòyìnbó.

The four of us uncovered his plot to turn Solari into his very own army in an attempt to take control of Nigeria. We had help from a band of Rogue Solari called Òmìnira, who had been trying to stop him for years. We're united now, Òmìnira and Solari, and are determined to undo all the harm Dr Dòyìnbó caused. Niyì, Hassan, Adanna and I form Nchebe, a group dedicated to protecting the academy and seeking out new Solari wherever they're discovered. It's been a lot to deal with, which is why we need a holiday. Adanna, however, doesn't seem to agree.

She closes the panel on the device and stands, brushing the sand from her cotton shorts. Her gaze shifts to the water and the two boys still playing amongst the waves.

'DAMI, activate ADA Rescue protocol,' Adanna says in a firm voice.

There's no answer from the AI that controls everything at the academy. I only know Adanna's command has been received when the clear blue sky above us suddenly darkens as angry clouds appear out of nowhere. A new chill fills the air, and I shiver at the sharp breeze now lashing me, picking up sand as it rushes towards the calm sea. The water responds to this attack in a defensive shrug, waves rising quickly in answering fury. Adanna has called up a storm, just as she'd planned.

I search for Hassan and Niyì in the water. Niyì's ice surfboard glides through it, cutting through the surging waves. Hassan is right beside him in his protective bubble, weaving through the water as the boys make their way back to the safety of the shore. Suddenly, the sea beneath Niyì begins to churn, bubbling like a pot boiling over. The violent movement shatters the ice surfboard and Niyì disappears, swallowed into the depths of the raging water. I suck in a sharp breath as the seconds tick by, until at last his head surfaces and he grabs hold of a broken piece of his board still floating on the surface.

Nearby, Hassan too is struggling, barely able to keep his protective shield in place as the massive waves crash into him. I don't move, even though my Ike rises to the surface and my hair drifts outwards, ready to spring into action.

Finally, Adanna blinks, and the drone above her rises higher in the air, its blades whirring as it surges forward, speeding towards the sea. She blinks again, her eyes adjusting to the video feed from the drone beaming straight into her brain. Its camera lens is now acting as her eyes through the power of her Ike. When the drone reaches Niyì, it stops directly above him as if waiting for further instructions.

Another blink, and this time the white-and-green device still resting on the sand flares to life. Its little legs scuttle forward at an unexpected speed, and when it hits the water, they retract and the solar-powered hover engine embedded inside it fires up, revealing what the device truly is – an oversized lifebuoy. Purpose-built for missions, it's controlled by Adanna's Ike and guided by the drone keeping watch over Niyì.

Adanna calls it RescuBot. As it zooms through the water towards its target, I know we're about to find out if it lives up to its name.

When RescuBot reaches Niyì, it slows down, swinging alongside him. The heavy waves batter it from all sides, but RescuBot is completely unbothered, moving closer until it's within grabbing distance. Niyì does so quickly, and once he's in place, the robotic buoy turns sharply, heading back towards the shore. Hassan, still safe inside his energy field, and the aerial drone are close behind. I glance at Adanna, but her face is a blank mask, even as RescuBot drags Niyì through the water, his body bouncing over the waves like a human beach ball.

They finally reach the shore and it takes Niyì a moment to stand, his long legs struggling to hold his weight. RescuBot's own little legs reappear and it scuttles back towards us. Niyì's gaze follows it, eventually reaching Adanna. I tense at the furious expression on his face.

'Adanna!' Niyì growls in warning as he strides towards us. Hassan scurries after him, trying but failing to hide his laughter.

Just like RescuBot, Adanna is unbothered, and a slow grin spreads over her face. It's the first emotion she's shown since we arrived.

'Good bot,' she croons, bending to pat the buoy when it reaches her. Then she straightens to face the other boy in front of her. 'That went well.'

Niyi's jaw drops.

CHAPTER
TWO

When Adanna decided to use HOME to test RescuBot, Niyì had volunteered to help, and Hassan and I decided to tag along. The idea of chilling on a deserted beach, even a virtual one, was too good to pass up. I reckon Niyì might be regretting his offer now.

'Some warning would have been nice,' Niyì mutters as he wipes water from his face.

Hassan bends down to examine RescuBot. 'Why una need dis tin sef?' he says in Pidgin English.

'Global water levels are rising because of climate change,' Adanna replies. 'That means an increased risk of flooding, especially in the Rivers Province area. We might be sent on water rescue missions in the future and I want us to be prepared.'

Niyì's eyebrows lift. 'Aren't you forgetting we have Ike?'

'We can't always rely on our powers.'

Niyì goes quiet because Adanna has a point. Our existence is still a huge secret from the general population, so we can't go around creating ice or energy shields whenever we feel like it. Solari are committed to helping Nigeria and its citizens, but we do it undercover because the world isn't ready to know about us yet.

'How far can RescuBot go?' I ask.

'As far as I can see him with the drone,' Adanna replies, her voice thick with pride. 'The drone can be used to carry RescuBot if necessary, and he can move three times as fast in the water as any human. He can also rescue up to six people at a time.'

'*He?*' Niyì asks. 'Don't you mean *it*.'

Adanna's only response is a sniff, and Niyì smirks back. Adanna's very touchy about her inventions and he knows that. He opens his mouth, ready to add more pepper, but the sound of doors opening behind me stops him and Niyì's face freezes.

I spin round to find my aunt, the new principal of the academy, standing in the open doorway. Beyond her stretches a brightly lit corridor, its harsh reality breaking the holographic spell of Ibeno Beach. Aunt Naomi steps inside, her long micro plaits swinging as she draws closer. A warm smile lights her face, but I sense worry behind her multicoloured eyes.

'I thought I might find you here, Nchebe.' Aunt Naomi glances around, finally noticing her tropical surroundings. Her smile turns rueful. 'I can understand why you want a break. I know things have been difficult since the Òmìnira joined us, but you've done me and the academy proud.'

Hassan grins and Niyì straightens, his chest puffing out at my aunt's words. Adanna rolls her eyes at him, and I barely stifle the giggle threatening to break free.

Aunt Naomi frowns suddenly. 'Where's Zahrah?'

'She's with Ògá Gbénga,' Adanna replies.

Zahrah is the newest member of Nchebe, but she visits her father, the former leader of the Òmìnira, on the weekends. My eyes narrow at my aunt. *She knows that*. Aunt Naomi makes a small distracted sound and Adanna pipes up.

'What's wrong?'

Aunt Naomi sighs. 'I have an urgent mission for the four of you.'

'Where?' I squeak.

'I dey hungry,' Hassan whines.

'When?' Niyì adds.

'Can I bring RescuBot?' Adanna demands.

The questions come thick and fast, and Hassan's is no surprise. He's always thinking about filling his belly.

Aunt Naomi laughs, her hands lifting as if to settle us. 'To think I was worried it was too soon.'

We haven't left the academy since we took down Dr Dòyìnbó, and as much as I love it here, it would be nice to see more of Nigeria.

Then my aunt's face sobers, the laughter dying. 'As you know, rainfall has been heavy lately.'

Hassan shrugs. 'E be rainy season.'

Aunt Naomi nods. 'Yes, but it's arrived early and this quantity of rain isn't normal.'

It's been raining non-stop for several weeks now. Not the cute drizzle we used to get in London, but a heavy, lashing rain that slaps you upside the head if you're silly enough to go outside in it. I haven't been living in Nigeria long enough to know how normal it is, but I heard that even the Councils, the two governing bodies that run Nigeria, are worried.

Adanna frowns. 'I told you, it's climate change, and it's getting worse every year.'

Aunt Naomi sighs. 'Regardless of the cause, the lower Niger River Basin has been severely impacted and the Councils have issued flood warnings across all of the southern provinces.'

'What does that have to do with us?' Niyì asks.

'The Iko dam in Cross River Province has been damaged and the immediate area surrounding it is at risk. When a flood warning is issued, communities in the affected area know they may have to evacuate at short notice. Normally, this isn't an issue, but there's one village that isn't responding to the alerts. It's isolated and dangerously close to the dam. We're worried it'll be destroyed if the dam breaks.'

Interest sparks in Adanna's face. 'Has this happened before? Maybe their communication system has been damaged.'

Aunt Naomi shakes her head. 'In previous years

they've always responded, even though they're very reclusive and shun almost all technology.'

Adanna's expression changes to horror. 'They don't like technology?' Then she shudders. 'Why?'

Aunt Naomi smiles at her reaction. 'They prefer a simpler way of life. One that's closer to how their ancestors lived. They're under the protection of the Councils, though it hasn't always been easy to maintain their isolation and keep the rest of the world away.'

'You want us to check the village out, don't you?' Niyì asks.

My aunt's smile drops. 'Yes. The villagers are wary of outsiders, but they've never rejected help before.' She sighs. 'In previous years the Councils would have sent the Protectors to investigate.'

I wince as it becomes clear why it has to be Nchebe. The Protectors were Solari who worked in the armed forces to help keep Nigeria and its citizens safe. But most of them are gone now because of Dr Dòyìnbó's schemes. The new Solari Force is replacing the role of the Protectors, but not for a few years when more students have graduated from the academy.

'No wahala,' Hassan says cheerfully. 'We go finish, quick, quick.'

Aunt Naomi nods, like she already knew we'd agree. 'I need you to keep a low profile. Your mission is simply to make contact, check the village received our warnings and, if so, find out why they haven't been responding.' Her face turns proper serious, and my stomach tightens. 'You'll need to win their trust. It's forbidden to bring technology into the village, and under no circumstances can they discover what you truly are.'

Rah! I think. If things get serious, how do we help without using our Ike or technology?

I glance at the others, knowing they must be wondering the same thing. But Adanna's already lost interest, her attention shifting back to RescuBot. Hassan has a big grin plastered on his face, his body flashing in and out of visibility as he struggles to hide his excitement. Then he disappears completely, the light patch of skin surrounding his left eye the last thing to vanish.

'Come back here,' Niyì snaps at Hassan. 'We've got a mission to prepare for.' He opens his hand and a small snowball forms.

Niyì doesn't hesitate, throwing it at the spot Hassan was last seen. The ball smacks into an invisible barrier and bounces off sharply. Hassan's energy shield ripples in response, and I catch a glimpse of his grinning face.

How are we supposed to keep a low profile?

CHAPTER THREE

The journey to Cross River Province only takes thirty minutes in the Gyrfalcon, our supersonic jet, so it's late morning by the time we arrive. We passed Iko dam on the way. Nestled into the surrounding hills, it's a clear path downhill from the dam to the village.

The rain beats a heavy rhythm outside, the sound loud even through the thick walls of the jet. It hasn't let up since we left Lagos. If anything, it's got heavier. We choose a landing spot close enough to walk to the village, but far enough to keep the Gyrfalcon hidden.

The forest is thick and humid around us, the rain pounding a constant chorus. Protected under plain black raincoats, we follow a narrow but well-worn path, dodging the huge puddles of murky brown water littering the ground. Every so often I catch Adanna staring nervously back the way we came. She's not a big fan of nature.

Soon we come to a small grove of oil palms. Their thick trunks shoot up from the ground, still short in their youth and topped by a heavy canopy of leafy fronds. Clustered near the base of the leaves, the distinctive bright red fruit grow in dense bunches. Many villages farm palm fruit in the Nigerian forests, taking care to do it sustainably, and with it they make red palm oil to sell.

A smell hits me all of a sudden – a mix of smoke and burning oil. It's strong and unpleasant. I recognize it from when my mum makes efo riro, a vegetable stew I love to eat with pounded yam. My nose twitches as I search for the source. It doesn't take long to find it. A little distance from the trees, thick steam curls from a metal barrel. Beneath it, a fire smoulders, and beside it is a shirtless middle-aged man wearing a red circular cap.

The man hasn't seen us yet. He's too busy pounding the palm fruit in the wooden bowl in front of him, the long stick in his hand twisting as it meets the bowl. I motion to the others and we stop. Adanna nods and steps forward, clearing her throat. The man jumps and holds the stick in front of him in defence. When he sees who we are, he lowers it, but only slightly.

'Who are you?' he demands, wiping rain from his eyes. 'What are you doing here?'

'We're sorry to intrude, but we're lost,' Adanna says softly. 'Can you help us?'

'How did you get here?' the man replies. His eyes dance about as if he's expecting more of us to burst out of the bush. 'You shouldn't be here.'

In the end, Aunt Naomi's plan was simple. We're posing as children on a school trip who have got separated from the main group. We're even wearing matching green uniforms beneath our raincoats. All we have to do is keep a lid on our powers. No drones, no disappearing, no ice and no telekinetic hair.

The man's expression grows even more suspicious as Adanna finishes explaining our cover story. 'Why don't you just call for help?' he sneers. 'Don't you city people all have phones?'

We're ready for this question too. In order to

strengthen our story and respect the villagers' views on technology, we left all our tech behind in the Gyrfalcon, including our only way to communicate with the academy and Aunt Naomi. Until we discover why the villagers haven't responded to the flood alerts, we're on our own.

'We left our bags behind, and our phones were inside,' Adanna replies in her most innocent voice. 'We've been walking for hours and we're scared.'

Her voice cracks a little on the last word, and the man's face softens. *I never knew Adanna was such a good actress.* The man glances around furtively, checking again that we are indeed alone. Then he pulls his cap from his head and scratches his bald head. Indecision dances across his face for a moment.

'My name is Ikenna,' he finally says.

We introduce ourselves quickly and Ikenna nods.

'You'd better follow me.'

The village feels curiously empty as we make our way through it. Abandoned buckets and containers surround the borehole where water is collected.

We pass several compounds – rectangular concrete buildings topped with corrugated iron roofs. Curtains twitch behind some windows, but no one comes out. There's a strange feeling of anticipation in the air, tinged with fear.

This continues until we arrive at a small compound with a rusted metal gate. Just beyond it, two small boys play in the rain. Half-dressed and soaking wet, their faces are lit with joy as they jump in and out of a big puddle guarding the entrance to the house. As soon as they spot us, they stop. Retreating quickly, their curious eyes follow our progress, even as they disappear into the unknown depths of the house. Ikenna ignores them, leading us inside too through a narrow corridor and cloth-covered doorway and into a small but clean living room. There's no TV or any other tech I'm so used to seeing. The furniture is worn and Ikenna motions us to sit.

'Can you help us get back to our group?' I ask quickly. 'We were leaving the area because of a flood warning when we got separated.'

Ikenna nods. 'Yes, we too have heard the warnings, but Afamefuna will protect us.'

Adanna and I share a look. *So they did receive the Councils' flood alert.* But why have they been ignoring it, and who the solar is Afamefuna?

'I'll have to petition on your behalf,' Ikenna adds, rubbing a hand across his face. 'I can't promise anything. Afamefuna is generous, but he's also strict.'

Before I can ask who this Afamefuna is, a small body darts into the room.

'Daddy!'

A little girl with solemn brown eyes throws herself at Ikenna. He catches her easily and they hug. Then she spins round, her eyes locking on to me.

'You sound strange,' the girl says shyly.

'I used to live in England,' I reply. 'I moved back to Nigeria recently.'

The girl opens her mouth to speak again, but her father's sharp voice stops her.

'Return to your bedroom, Nneka.'

Nneka straightens guiltily. With a quick glance at me, she begins to retreat back the way she came. Ikenna's hand lifts, landing gently on her head. A moment passes between them and I'm reminded of my own papa and the power of his reassuring touch. I understand now why Ikenna is helping us, despite his obvious reluctance. We're children, at the end of the day. A pang of guilt races through me at our deception.

'Does anyone have a phone or computer we can use to contact our school?' Adanna asks.

Ikenna swallows, his eyes darting towards the window again.

'Afamefuna has forbidden contact with outsiders.'

Is that why Ikenna seems so nervous? Whoever this person is, he seems to have a strange hold over the village.

'Who be Afamefuna?' Hassan asks, voicing the unspoken question.

'He's our protector. Since he arrived in our village, our crops have flourished and our people have remained safe. He is Arusi.'

The Igbo word is unfamiliar to me, but Adanna speaks it and understands the meaning instantly. Her body goes stiff and her mouth drops open.

'What's the matter?' I whisper. 'What's Arusi?'

A look passes between Ikenna and Adanna. An expression of devoted pride spreads across his face as confusion blossoms on hers.

'A god,' Adanna finally replies, her tone careful. 'He's saying there's a god living in this village.'

Ikenna stands and his shoulders straighten. 'Come. Afamefuna is waiting.'

CHAPTER FOUR

We're the ones waiting.

After we left Ikenna's house, he led us through the village in the pouring rain. I was already soaked, so I hardly noticed. The village is small, eight houses in total, and it didn't take long for me to realize they're laid out in an irregular circle. Ikenna's house is at the bottom edge, and as we made our way into the centre of the village, the missing villagers lined the way, watching us silent and unblinking. It made my skin crawl, their stares reminding me of when I lived in England and all anyone ever looked at was my hair as if I was some sort of exhibit.

At last we came to the village hall, easily the largest

and tallest of the buildings. Unlike the others, it has a flat roof with wide drains, and water dripped down the sides of its reddish walls, pooling into a shallow moat surrounding the entrance. Ikenna led us inside through several corridors and into a room. The worried-looking villagers followed, and we've all been waiting here since.

The room is large. A rectangular space with bare floors and even barer walls. Metal torches line them, their naked flames illuminating the room and casting an eerie glow over everything. Near the wall furthest from us rests a single wooden chair, set apart like a throne. It's empty and plain, yet it holds the attention of every adult here. We're the only children in the room, and the message is very clear. *We are not wanted here.* A prickle of fear skates across my skin.

A low murmur amongst the villagers breaks the silence. The prickle intensifies as a boy enters the room. He's taller than Niyì and dressed in a patterned dansiki shirt over plain black trousers, just like the other village men. He doesn't pause, making his way instead to the front of the room where the wooden chair rests. He takes a seat, and as he crosses his arms,

I get a flash of the beaded bracelet wrapped round his right wrist. I also get my first proper view of the boy's face.

Upturned eyes framed by thick lashes sit above a strong nose. The cleft in his chin is a deep slash, partly hidden by the patchy shadow of hair dusting his cheeks. He can't be more than fifteen, despite his attempts to look older. Yet there's an air of authority about him that makes me want to stand up straighter. *Is this their god?*

There's no smile on the boy's wide mouth as he turns to Ikenna and spreads his hands in invitation. Ikenna steps forward and pulls his cap from his head. 'Thank you for seeing me, Afamefuna. These children are lost, and they need our help.'

Afamefuna is fully frowning now. 'Have you forgotten that we do not deal with outsiders? They cannot be trusted.'

I try not to look offended at his words, but beside me Adanna is failing miserably.

'They're children in need of help.' Ikenna's voice is pleading. 'Just like you when you first arrived here.'

Someone gasps, and an ominous silence settles

over the room. I wonder again how this boy has so much power over fully grown adults. The tension is so thick and Adanna winces from the pressure of all the emotions flying about. I reach out and touch her shoulder. She gives me an answering smile through gritted teeth. My attention returns to Afamefuna to find him eyeing Ikenna with a wolfish smile.

'And since I arrived, have your farms not improved? Your lives become easier?' he asks in a soft tone. 'Have I not proven my worth to this village time and time again?'

I frown at Afamefuna's stilted words. It's as if he's deliberately trying to sound older.

Ikenna twists the cap in his hands. 'Of course you have, and we're grateful.'

'Then why did you break my one rule and bring these strangers here?'

I step forward quickly, unable to stand the tension any longer.

'It's not Ikenna's fault. We didn't give him much choice.'

Afamefuna smiles, but there's no humour in it. 'There is always a choice, and I have made mine.'

'Please—' Ikenna begins, but Afamefuna is no longer listening to him.

He raises his hands and the lit torches surrounding the room flare brighter. It's followed by a loud *whoosh* as smaller balls of fire break away and begin circling the room. The temperature rises, an ominous threat swirling in the air, and sweat breaks out on my top lip as fear races through me. *I understand now why they think he's a god.*

'The four of you must leave and never return,' Afamefuna roars.

A group of villagers near him huddle down as if they already know what's coming. Then a thick arrow of roaring flames bursts towards Ikenna from a torch in the corner of the room. It stops just before it reaches him, then spins away sharply, looking for new prey. From the corner of my eye, I spot a red glow blazing in our direction.

'Get down,' Niyì shouts, pulling me to the floor.

Around us, frightened villagers scream, and more flames arc through the air in a blazing pyrotechnic display. The heat intensifies and I struggle to breathe, my chest heaving with effort. Afamefuna is standing now, his hands moving in the air like a conductor. The flames respond obediently, his willing orchestra. That's when it hits me.

'He's no god!' I gasp. 'He's Solari.'

Afamefuna's narrowed eyes find me, and the flames surrounding us burn even brighter. I swallow hard. He's a very powerful Solari. *But what kind?* He can't be an Emitter, like Niyì and Hassan. He isn't making fire, only controlling it. There's a curious calm about him too that feels out of place in the terrifying chaos. Then I realize he's not actually trying to hurt us. This is all for show. *He's trying to scare us away!*

The veins in Afamefuna's neck bulge and the skin round his eyes glows a peculiar orange as he beckons a ball of fire towards him. It answers, spinning through the air in an awesome display of power until it hovers above his hand.

'There's only one way to end this.'

Niyì's voice is a low ominous sound, and I know immediately what he plans to do. Aunt Naomi's warning about revealing our powers rings in my head, but before I can stop him, Niyì stands. Afamefuna's head twists his way immediately. The ball of fire in

31

his hand spins in place for a moment, then suddenly it's whizzing towards us. I hold my breath as the fiery sphere keeps coming until suddenly it freezes in mid-air. I'm mesmerized by the sound of water popping and hissing as steam fills the air and the sphere evaporates. Niyì grins, an icy-blue mist leaking from his hands. Afamefuna's body stiffens, and his eyes widen momentarily. The glare he gives Niyì makes anger swirl in my belly, and Ike itches across my scalp. There's no point in pretending any more, so I stand too and let my power ignite.

My braids uncoil from their bantu knots, erupting around me in a defiant arc. Adanna is beside me then, her body coiled and ready to fight. Next to her, Hassan raises his energy shield, a hard expression on his face. I stare back at Afamefuna, daring him to try us. But he surprises me. His hands drop, and immediately the flames disappear, as if snuffed out by some unseen hand.

'Every villager is to leave and forget what they saw here.'

Afamefuna's voice is soft, but the command in it is loud. It batters my mind, demanding obedience.

My body tenses, unsure whether to obey or not, and I frown, confused that I'm even considering it. The adults lining the room don't hesitate though. They stiffen as one, then file out of the room, Ikenna included. An icy feeling dances down my spine. *I've seen people act like this before.* It's what happens whenever my papa or aunt use their Ike. They're mind benders and can control people's minds and memories.

Afamefuna must be a Psionic, just like them . . .

CHAPTER
FIVE

'Tell me. What is Solari?' Afamefuna demands, command heavy in his voice.

'He's a mind bender,' I hiss to the others urgently. 'You need to strengthen your mental defences.'

Niyì's eyes widen, but he doesn't argue. Neither does Hassan or Adanna. A while back, Aunt Naomi taught Nchebe how to protect our minds from Solari with telepathic powers. It's mandatory training at the academy now, and students are taught to always have mental defences up just in case. It's not enough though; I've never felt Ike this powerful before.

'Did you see what he was doing with the fire?' Niyì mutters. 'I've never seen your aunt or dad do that.'

Hassan looks worried. 'I think say he go get telekinetic powers too.'

I glance at Adanna and her face is stiff. So Afamefuna has two Ike, just like her. There aren't too many Solari like that around as most of us only have the one.

'What is a Solari?'

Afamefuna's voice is louder this time and the power in it has my head snapping back towards him. I can feel the strings of his Ike trying to latch on to my mind. I grit my teeth, strengthening my mental shield.

'Stop doing that,' I snap at him.

Afamefuna blinks. 'My power doesn't work on you?' His gaze moves from me to the others, assessing each of us. 'Who are you?'

The compulsion is gone from his voice, leaving only shock. I exhale sharply as the pressure in my head eases.

Niyì steps forward. 'That's what we should be asking you.'

The two boys face off against each other, neither willing to back down. After a moment, Afamefuna closes his eyes. When he opens them again, the sadness there is enough to make me flinch.

'My name is Afamefuna, but you can call me Afam,' he begins quietly. 'I was born in Enugwu Ukwu, and everything was fine until I turned six and my powers appeared. My frightened parents abandoned me, and I've been moving from place to place since, scared that my secret would eventually be discovered. For years I did this, always alone, until I came here and the villagers accepted me.' Then he sighs. 'I'm sorry about earlier. But you wouldn't believe how many people come here with questionable intentions. When I first arrived, the village was a mess. Outsiders took advantage of the villagers' dislike of technology and would loot or try to steal land.'

'Una don dey help dem?' Hassan moves closer, curiosity getting the better of him.

Afam shrugs. 'I've always struggled to understand why I was cursed with my powers until I arrived here and realized I could use them to help others.'

Afam gestures at us, as if to say, *Your turn*. The four of us share a quick look. We never expected to find a new Solari on this mission. There hasn't been one since me. I still remember how confusing it was in the early days, and a flash of sympathy for Afam hits me. I nod and the others understand immediately without any need for words. I turn back to Afam and take a deep breath. Then I begin, explaining what it means to be Solari and what the Academy of the Sun means to us. Finally, I tell him Ike isn't a curse, but a blessing. One that makes us unique but also brings with it a heavy responsibility.

'I'm Solari?' Afam breathes, an expression of wonder lighting up his face. 'I always thought I was the only one like me.'

'No way.' Niyì laughs, relaxing now things have calmed down. 'There are hundreds of us back at the academy.'

Hassan slaps Afam on the back, eager to make friends as usual. 'You go enjoy de place well, well.'

Afam's head tilts. 'What do you mean?'

'Now we've found you, we have to take you back to the academy with us.' Adanna is more careful, and she watches Afam closely as she speaks. 'It's the agreement the Councils made with Principal Naomi. All Solari must live and train at the academy.'

Alarm flashes across Afam's face. 'I'm not going anywhere.' Then he takes a quick step back. 'This village is my home, and its people are my family. They need me.'

'We don't use Ike on family,' Adanna snaps. 'As long as you're using your powers to control them, they're your prisoners.'

Afam looks away, unable to meet Adanna's accusing stare.

'Why are you letting them think you're a god?' I ask, my tone gentle. 'My mum says God doesn't take away choice. It's wrong what you're doing.'

'I never said I was one,' Afam protests. 'They assumed, and I didn't bother to correct them. It's easier when everyone listens to me.' He rubs his arm, his tone turning defensive. 'My powers keep us safe.'

'You're not strong enough to protect the villagers from what's coming,' I say. My head tilts curiously. 'Why have you been ignoring the flood warnings?'

Afam stiffens. 'Outsiders can't be trusted. They lie and they break promises.'

'The messages from the Councils aren't lies,' Niyì replies, ever protective of Nigeria's leaders. 'Iko dam was damaged in the last storm and there's a risk it could burst. The villagers need to prepare for a possible evacuation.'

'Evacuation?' Afam's eyes widen.

'E means say you must dey ready to leave.' Hassan's expression is full of sympathy.

Afam steps back, a new wariness now visible on his face. 'No one is leaving. This is our home and I will protect it.'

'You'll fail,' Niyì snaps, losing patience. 'We were sent here to help, but we can't do that if you won't let us.'

Niyì's voice rises on the last word and Adanna places a hand on his arm. She gives a quick shake of her head, and I wonder what she's sensing from Afam. I find out when he replies, his own voice rising.

'You've already lied about being lost schoolchildren. How do I know this story about a special academy and broken dam isn't just another lie?'

'It's not,' I declare, willing Afam to believe me. 'We're trying to protect the village.'

He shakes his head. 'That's what others before you have said, right before they tried to steal our land or force us to use technology.'

Adanna slowly steps closer, like she's trying not to spook Afam. 'I get why you're scared, but we're not those people.' Her voice is low and soothing.

'I've heard that before too.' Afam's eyes go hard. 'I've finally found a place where I belong and I will not abandon it.'

Afam closes his eyes, and suddenly the doors behind us swing open. One by one, villagers pour into the room, Ikenna included. Each one wears a vacant look on their face that tells me they're once again under Afam's influence. Like mindless zombies, they surround him, forming what looks suspiciously like a human shield.

'You're powerful, and together you might be able to force me to leave, but are you prepared to hurt them to achieve that?' He gestures to the room full of people. 'They'll do whatever I say, and I say we're staying.'

Niyi's hands lift, icy mist already blooming, but I shake my head at him. We can't risk breaking Aunt Naomi's rule again. We already got lucky once when

40

Afam wiped the villagers' memories. Niyì's hand drops reluctantly, and the mist fades away. Afam nods as if we've come to an unspoken agreement. Then, without another word, he walks away, his zombified entourage following.

CHAPTER
SIX

We stay in that room for hours, trying to figure out what to do next. The dam could burst at any moment, and without a way of contacting Aunt Naomi, we won't know when. Meanwhile, the weather outside has only been growing worse. I eye the window and the rain still beating down on the other side of it. I don't think time is on our side.

'What are we going to do?' Niyì asks for the fifth time as he takes a seat in Afam's chair. Adanna throws him a glare and he returns it. 'I'm going to keep asking until we come up with a plan.'

Hassan whistles low under his breath. 'Na wa. Dat guy dey vex too much.'

'Afam is in pain,' Adanna says, her voice sharp. 'That would make most people angry too.'

Niyì snorts and crosses his legs. 'You mean *he* is a pain.'

Adanna shakes her head. 'I'm serious. I've never sensed so much hurt coming from someone before. Whatever happened to Afam in the past, it's still affecting him.'

Niyì rolls his eyes at her. 'We all have a past. It's not an excuse to behave like that.'

'Guys,' Hassan begins in a hesitant voice.

Adanna ignores him, her eyebrow lifting in challenge. 'Really, Niyì? I remember you being very annoying not too long ago.'

I snort, trying to hold back my laughter as I think about how difficult Niyì was after he lost his Ike a few months ago when he was trying to protect me from Dr Dòyìnbó. Luckily, my father was able to get his Ike back.

Niyì folds his arms across his chest. 'That was different.'

'Guys, wahala dey o!' Hassan's tone is sharper this time.

43

'What?' Niyì snaps.

Hassan points to the closed door in the corner. 'E normal say water dey enter de house?'

Confused, I follow his finger, only to gasp at the sight of the water rushing through the gap beneath the door. Niyì jumps up from the chair and the others move back as it snakes its away across the ground. We all share a look, knowing we've run out of time.

We race outside to find the village in total chaos. Heavy wind batters the surrounding trees. Villagers scatter about, their frantic bodies barely visible through the thick downpour. There's so much shouting, though it's barely audible above the roar of the rising water that's already ankle-deep. Ikenna dashes past, panic etched on his face. By his side are the two boys we saw earlier, each desperately clinging on to him.

'Have you seen Nneka?' Ikenna asks another villager.

The woman nods, then points to a lone figure, before she too disappears in the shadowy curtain of rain. Afam is standing there. One arm is cradled around Nneka, the other is lifted as he tries to control the thick tree trunk barrelling towards them. A sharp breath leaves me, and I step forward to help. It isn't needed though. Afam's arm shakes, but his hold on Nneka doesn't waver. Then, just before the tree trunk reaches them, it stops and swings sharply to the right, landing with a splash a safe distance away.

'Thank you,' Ikenna gasps when he reaches them and takes Nneka into his arms.

Afam nods at him, then stiffens. His gaze shifts, finding the four of us, and his mouth tightens. 'I thought you would have left by now.'

'We're not here to fight with you,' Adanna replies. 'We really do want to help.'

Afam stares at us for a long minute. Then he sighs. 'We need to get everyone to higher ground.'

He's right – but how? The land around us slopes downwards. I eye the trees peeking above the top of the village hall. They're too far away and too tall to climb. *Wait ... the hall!*

'I have an idea,' I gasp.

Without waiting for a reply, I turn towards the discarded tree trunk that's already started to float away in the water. Ike rises in me and I send out two thick bolts of hair. They wrap round the trunk, lifting it into the air. I quickly place it against the side of the building and turn, already looking for another big piece of wood. I find one easily and repeat the movement, positioning it parallel to the first. It takes a moment for the others to catch on, but when they do, they rush to help.

Piece by piece, we erect a makeshift ramp, and Niyì uses his Ike to freeze it all together, and soon there's a brand-new walkway leading all the way up to the roof of the village hall.

'Quickly,' Afam shouts.

The water is now thigh-deep, making it difficult to move. It takes all five of us to herd the dozen plus villagers up the ramp, one at a time. Again and again we do this until at last all the villagers are safe. By this point the water has reached our waists.

'Let's go,' Niyì shouts.

Afam nods and closes his eyes. Using telekinesis, he rises into the air, floating upwards until he reaches the roof.

'Show-off,' Niyì mutters under his breath before ascending the ramp.

Adanna is next and she follows him, Hassan close behind her. I bring up the rear, but as I start the climb, something in the water crashes into the base of the ramp, making it shake. I squeeze my eyes shut as I wait for it to stop. Niyì, Adanna and Hassan reach the roof, leaving me on the ramp alone.

'Come on, Onyeka,' Adanna bellows, a ferocious gust of wind almost drowning her out. 'You're almost there.'

I look down and really wish I hadn't. As I scoot forward again, my feet slip on the wet wood and I lose my footing, sliding off the ramp. Adanna screams as my hair stretches out, clamps down on a branch and breaks my fall. The ramp wobbles, unwilling to hold my weight any longer, and I hang there by my hair.

I let Ike rise again, and with a heavy grunt, I send another bolt of wet hair towards one of the gutters lining the roof. But before my hair can reach it, the ramp tilts as the water rushing beneath me dislodges it completely. My hair touches the smooth metal, a desperate graze, and then I'm falling. A cry leaves my lips as I tumble towards the ground.

CHAPTER
SEVEN

My cry cuts off abruptly when my body comes to a sudden stop. I'm hovering above the ground, held up by a power that's definitely not mine. Afam's eyes are locked on me, his right hand stretched out in my direction.

Beside him, Niyì, Hassan and Adanna's impressed faces grow more so as Afam curls his hand and I drift towards him like a helium balloon on a string. I don't enjoy the experience, and when I reach the roof, my legs wobble for a second before I find my balance. I nod at Afam, grateful, though surprised.

'Thanks,' I say, my voice a breathless rush.

Afam doesn't reply, his gaze now fixed on

something behind me. His expression quickly morphs into one of growing horror. Then I hear it – the dull roar of rushing water. I turn to see a solid wall of it, easily three storeys high, charging towards the village. The massive wave sweeps aside everything in its path, gobbling up trees and land like a hungry beast. The villagers start screaming, the sound of their fear a loud chorus.

'We need to get out of here,' Adanna yells. 'It's a tsunami.'

'How?' Niyì asks. 'We're trapped!'

'Stay together,' Afam shouts, and the villagers obey immediately, huddling into a tight ball.

Niyì, Hassan, Adanna and I form our own little huddle, our hands grasping one another tightly. This is beyond even our powers. Afam ignores us and instead stretches out his hand as a look of concentration falls over his face. The giant wave is almost upon us and I flinch, bracing for impact . . . but it never comes.

Instead, the giant wave crashes against some unseen barrier. I suck in a sharp breath as the water flows sideways, its onward path now blocked. It follows its new route, circling the outer edges of the village in its destructive quest. Afam has created a telekinetic dam, allowing the water to pass us by.

'I can't hold it much longer,' Afam hisses. Sweat beads his face, his jaw clenched as he struggles to carry the burden alone.

Hassan steps forward immediately and lifts his hand. A yellow energy shield appears in front of Afam's invisible one, strengthening it. Together, they hold back the devastating wave, but I eye the churning water with worry. It isn't enough, and our Ike isn't limitless. We need something more permanent to hold back the water.

My eyes meet Niyì's and it's clear he realizes this as well. He joins Afam and Hassan, his own hand outstretched, and his Ike combines with the other two. Tendrils of frost appear, racing along the telekinetic and energy barrier. They mould themselves to it, forming into a solid wall of ice that begins to surround the small village in a horseshoe shape.

'Hurry!' Afam whispers, his outstretched hand beginning to shake.

Niyì grits his teeth. 'I'm doing my best.'

My heart races. There are just two houses left

unprotected, and Niyì's ice rushes to enclose them as the last of Afam's strength gives out. Just in time too – without Afam's power, Hassan's energy shield is no match for the powerful wave, and the built-up water slams into the ice wall. The ice shifts, straining against the sheer volume of liquid. I hold my breath—

Seconds pass, and the wall creaks and shifts under the pressure . . .

Then minutes, as tiny cracks begin to appear . . .

But the ice holds.

Shouts of joy ring out from the relieved villagers when they realize they're finally safe. With the flow of water from the burst dam now blocked off, the water still trapped within the village begins to calm, and my body relaxes for the first time in hours.

'Nneka!'

Ikenna's sudden shout is followed by a splash that makes my body tighten again. I follow his horrified gaze to find Nneka down below, her small head disappearing beneath the body of water that still surrounds the village.

'Save her, Afam,' Ikenna pleads.

Afam stares at him helplessly. He's too drained.

I reach for Ike, my hair lengthening instantly, and I search for Nneka in the moving water. A moment later, her head pops back up, her hands lifted as she tries to stay afloat. I stretch out my hair, trying to latch on to the little girl, but the water carries her further away, beyond the reach of my power. I grit my teeth, my whole body straining as I try again. But it's no use.

I turn back to the others, desperate. That's when I notice Adanna's eyes are closed. The next second, a familiar shape appears in the sky above us, its blades whirring as it speeds towards Nneka. But it's the green-and-white robot suspended from it that has my attention. Adanna opens her eyes and RescuBot drops through the air, entering the water with a loud splash. Its engines are already on and it zooms through the water towards its target.

When RescuBot reaches Nneka, it slows down, swinging alongside her. Instinctively Nneka grabs the robotic buoy. Once she's secure, RescuBot heads back to the village hall with the aerial drone close behind. When Nneka is once again within reach, I use my Ike, easily grabbing hold of her this time. I lift her back up to the roof and into the waiting arms of her father. Ikenna scoops her up, his arms tightening like he never plans to let go of her again.

Niyì turns to Adanna. 'How did you—?'

'I activated the drone and RescuBot when we made our way to the village hours ago,' she cuts in quickly. 'I used Ike to hide them in the forest nearby.' She shrugs. 'I thought we might need them.'

'Na wa!' Hassan breathes. 'I happy say e don work.'

Me too! It explains why Adanna seemed so nervous on our way here. It's so typical of her to be several steps ahead.

Afam drops down from exhaustion onto the iron roof beneath us and we join him. The water below us is already slowing, now that its supply has been cut off. I eye the massive ice wall Niyì, Afam and Hassan created. It's the only thing separating us from disaster. Then my gaze shifts to the relieved villagers clustered on top of the roof. Soaking and tired, but safe. I don't know how, but we did it.

Actually, I do. We did it together.

CHAPTER EIGHT

Night comes and goes as we wait for the water to recede within the village. It's cramped on the roof and everyone is too tense and worried to sleep. Then someone starts singing an old folk song. A second voice joins, then a third, and soon everyone is singing as one song turns into another.

Time passes much quicker after that, and the first rays of the sun reveal the full extent of the devastation. Though most buildings remain standing, the water still flowing beneath us is littered with debris. A fallen tree floats past a football like strange playmates. Once the water recedes enough to safely wade through, we help the villagers down from the roof.

'I no believe say we survive am,' Hassan says, shock still lacing his voice.

'We almost didn't,' I reply.

'Because of me.' Afam's face is a pinched mask as he surveys the wreckage. 'I should have listened to the flood warnings.'

'Yes,' Adanna says softly. 'But you also saved everyone,' she adds.

'If you hadn't come –' Afam swallows hard – 'I don't even want to think about what would have happened.'

Neither do I. The villagers cluster around the hall, whispering in hushed voices. Each face is so different and yet familiar in the same sad and exhausted expression they all wear. But there's hope there too, and most of it is directed our way. Then it hits me why. *They think we're gods like Afam.* Unease slithers down my spine.

'How are we going to explain ourselves to them?' Niyi whispers, catching on quickly.

'Don't worry,' Afam replies. 'I'll take care of it.' He closes his eyes. 'After I leave, you will forget me and all you have seen in the last two days.'

Around us, the villagers go still as their faces

freeze into blank stares as Afam weaves new memories for them.

'There was a flash flood and you all survived by staying on the roof of the village hall.' Afam's eyes open and his attention moves back to us. 'They will remember none of what happened here.'

Niyì winces but says nothing.

'What will happen to the village now?' Adanna asks.

Afam sighs. 'The villagers will rebuild, like they always do.'

'You said you were leaving?' I ask hopefully. 'Does that mean . . . ?'

Afam nods. 'It's time.'

Relief fills me. 'I'm glad you've changed your mind about the academy.'

'We should go before they come round,' Niyì says, eyeing the villagers. 'Principal Naomi will be worried sick by now.'

Afam steps back. 'I'm not coming with you.'

My eyes fly to his face. 'What? But you said—'

'I don't deserve a place at the academy,' Afam interrupts. 'Look at what almost happened here. I'm a danger to others.'

'No,' I insist. I can't let him do this. 'You made a mistake, and that's exactly why you should come with us. The academy exists so we can learn and do better.'

'I should know,' Niyì adds. 'I made a huge mistake that lost me my family, but I found a new one at the academy.'

Afam's lips lift in a smile, but there's something wrong with it. It doesn't match the look of regret in his eyes. 'You will forget all that happened in this village.' His tone is a deep growl that scrapes along my nerves like nails on a chalkboard. 'You will forget who I am and all mention of my name.'

I'm so busy focusing on the jarring sensation that I almost miss the power of Afam's Ike as it slips past my defences. By the time I notice, it's already taking effect, and my mind suddenly grows heavy. It takes all my strength not to fall into the deep pit of nothingness. A quick glance at the others tells me I'm not the only one. Niyì, Hassan and Adanna have gone still, their faces blank.

'What are you doing?' I push out through tight lips.

'I'm sorry, but I can't come with you. This is the only way I know how to protect everyone.' Afam frowns.

'Your mental defences are good, but all I needed was more time to understand how I could get past them. You won't remember any of this after I'm gone, and for that I'm sorry. But know this, I am for ever changed from meeting you all, and I promise I'll earn the right to join you at the Academy of the Sun one day.'

'Please don't do this,' I whisper, even as I feel the renewed press of Afam's power against my weakening defences.

Afam doesn't respond. Instead, he lifts his hand and removes the beaded bracelet wrapped round his wrist. I'm helpless to stop him as he takes my hand and slips it on.

His eyes bore into mine. 'I will return for this.'

Then everything goes black.

'Onyeka!'

I blink at the sound of Aunt Naomi's voice. Her concerned face is pressed up close to mine and I take a startled step back. The world comes into sharp focus, revealing a village devastated by a flood and a bunch of equally confused people that I've never seen before.

In the distance, Council soldiers dismount from two helicopters hovering above the water. Closer in, even more of them are scattered about, tending to the villagers. One of them, a bald man, looks familiar . . . *Iken something?* A pounding begins in my head as I try to process it all. How did I get here? Where's Niyì, Hassan and . . . ?

'Adanna?' I cry, my body shaking.

'It's okay,' my aunt says in a soothing voice. 'She's right here. They're all here.'

I follow her pointing hand, only then noticing the three of them clustered together a little way behind her. I rush over, the calf-high water slowing me down. Adanna turns to greet me and we hug. I don't complain when she squeezes too tightly. Niyì gives me a nod, and I pretend not to notice that Hassan's smile is strained.

'What happened?' I ask, pulling away from Adanna as Aunt Naomi joins us. Adanna shrugs.

'I was hoping you'd know the answer to that question,' my aunt replies. 'I've been trying to contact you for almost a day. First to warn you about the dam. Then after it burst to check on your safety. I feared the worst after I heard no word from you all.' Her

eyes drift over the four of us. 'I remotely recalled the
Gyrfalcon back to the academy before the waters hit,
and once it was safe to do so, hurried here. When we
arrived, we found the four of you and the villagers just
standing there in a strange daze.'

Her gaze shifts to the icy wall surrounding the
village. 'We also found *that*. What happened here?'

I shake my head, but my thoughts and memories
are a jumbled mess.

'I-I don't know.'

Niyì stands. 'Did you say it's been a day since we
left the academy?'

Aunt Naomi nods.

'That's impossible – we only just arrived. We were
with that man –' Niyì points at the bald man I spotted
earlier – 'I think.'

'Me?' he squeaks. 'I have never met you before.'

I reach up to rub my forehead and my gaze catches
on a strange beaded bracelet wrapped round my wrist.
Where did that come from? I remember us arriving
in the Gyrfalcon, meeting the man in the forest, but
everything is hazy from then onwards. That only
happened a few minutes ago ... *didn't it?*

'This is all very irregular,' Aunt Naomi says. 'The four of you seem to have lost your memory of the twenty-four-hour period shortly after your arrival, and the villagers don't remember the last two days.'

I frown. 'Like a mass amnesia event?'

'Maybe some tin don knock all of us for head?' Hassan rubs his scalp, as if checking for a lump.

Adanna looks doubtful. 'At the same time?'

'Maybe there was some sort of sonic wave then?' Niyì offers.

'Yet you successfully completed your mission.' Aunt Naomi pauses. 'Something very strange happened here though.'

'Or *someone*?' Adanna says slowly.

I stare at her. 'What do you mean?'

'Niyì and Hassan are strong, but if the dam burst, there's no way they could have created that barrier quickly enough to stop a tsunami,' Adanna says. 'A very powerful someone must have helped them.'

'Like a secret superhero?' Niyì laughs, but I hear the confusion in his voice.

Aunt Naomi gives her a considered look. 'You

think this mysterious person also has something to do with your missing memories?'

Adanna nods. I glance down at the beaded bracelet again. *Is she right?* Someone has gone to a lot of trouble to hide whatever happened here. Yet they left me this clue. *Why?*

Niyì points to the long wall of ice surrounding the village.

'How are you going to explain that to the villagers?'

Aunt Naomi grimaces. 'They don't like trouble, so hopefully they won't ask too many questions.'

'What una dey tell de Councils?' Hassan asks her.

'I don't know, but it's not important right now. My first priority is getting you children home.'

Home . . . the Academy of the Sun.

But something niggles at the back of my mind. A tiny voice that whispers I'm forgetting something important. Aunt Naomi turns to lead the way to the helicopters. Niyì, Hassan and Adanna also follow, but I pause, my gaze drawn back to the towering wall. It feels wrong to leave.

'Are you coming?'

I turn to find Adanna watching me, an unreadable

expression on her face. Something tells me I'm going to have a lot of questions to answer later. I just wish I had some answers. The bracelet suddenly feels heavy round my wrist and I sigh.

'Yes. Let's go home.'

Happy
World Book Day!

When you've read this book, you can keep the fun going by swapping it, talking about it with a friend, or reading it again!

What do you want to read next? Whether it's **comics**, **audiobooks**, **recipe books** or **non-fiction** you can visit your school, local library or nearest bookshop for your next read – someone will always be happy to help.

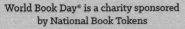

World Book Day is about changing lives through reading

When you **choose to read** in your spare time it makes you

| Feel happier | Better at reading | More successful |

Find your **reading superpower** by

1. **Listening to books being read aloud (or listening to audiobooks)**
2. **Having books at home**
3. **Choosing the books YOU want to read**
4. **Asking for ideas on what to read next**
5. **Making time to read**
6. **Finding ways to make reading FUN!**

SPONSORED BY

Changing lives through a love of books and reading.

World Book Day® is a charity sponsored by National Book Tokens

ILLUSTRATED BY VIVIAN TRUONG

HAVE YOU READ ALL OF THE EPIC ONYEKA BOOKS?

TURN THE PAGE TO READ
AN EXCITING EXTRACT FROM
ONYEKA AND THE ACADEMY OF THE SUN!

'Onyeka!'

I flinch, a prickle spreading across my scalp as Cheyenne's impatient voice cuts through the panic rising in me.

'Come *on*, fam! While it's still 2025.'

The already stuffy heat of the changing room grows hotter and the sharp smell of chlorine stings my nose. I feel like throwing up.

'I'm not coming out,' I mutter at the thick, wooden door separating us.

A quick shuffle of feet, followed by a sharp knock. 'The pool's gonna close at this rate,' Cheyenne replies without any sympathy. 'Have you got it on?'

I stare at the swimming cap Mum insisted I wear, resting on the floor where I threw it. I knew it was going to cause me problems.

'It won't fit,' I say. 'I tried already. My hair's too big.'

Cheyenne makes a noise that sounds both like a sigh and grunt . . . a *srunt*. 'Can't you just ditch it?'

I snort back. 'You know what Mum will do if my hair gets loose or wet.'

'She won't find out,' Cheyenne replies. But we both hear the lie in her voice. Mum always finds out. It's her superpower.

'I'm not coming out,' I repeat, but there's a wobble in my voice that gives me away. I'm no match for Cheyenne.

She knows it too and pounces immediately, like a cheetah from one of the wildlife documentaries Mum loves. We watch them together the rare times she isn't working.

'Open up,' Cheyenne hollers, and the whole changing room grows silent around us.

My belly tightens. I hate it when Cheyenne does that. Just because she loves attention, doesn't mean I do too. The already tiny space of the cubicle closes in around me and my chest tightens, making it difficult to breathe. Energy surges across my skin, but I force it back down. I can't get upset. I am absolutely not allowed to lose control. It's Mum's number one rule.

I remember the first time I felt like this. Mum and I were waiting hand in hand at a bus stop and a group of kids started making fun of my hair. Mum ignored them, then bent down to me, as if she knew I was about to lose it. Her smile was gentle as she told me that I needed to control my emotions because bad things would happen if I ever set them free.

This was before she taught me the Fibonacci numbers that help keep my emotions in check. Apparently, it's some mathematical sequence from ancient India, but someone decided to name it after an Italian guy. It works though. It's hard to lose your temper when you're trying to remember what the next number is.

I close my eyes now and start counting, running through the numbers as I try to calm down.

Zero . . .

One . . .

With each number, I trace the shape in my mind, giving it a colour, texture and taste.

Zero is a rough-edged blue and tastes like waffles, no syrup.

One I give a shiny orange with the sharp tang of vinegar.

Bit by bit, the prickle under my skin goes away, but I continue to count, just to be safe.

I'm back to number *one* again. This time it's brown and squishy, but with the rich flavour of the doughnuts Mum never lets me have.

Two is a hazy, dull grey. Completely boring and *normal*.

I stop counting as number *two* does the trick and my racing heart begins to slow. The door handle rattles and I jump. I'd forgotten about Cheyenne. I unlock the heavy door and she slips in wearing a blue swimsuit. Her face is shiny, and I can smell the coconut oil wafting from it. She always uses too much. Even in her hair. Today, she's pulled it into a short Afro puff, held in place by a red, stretchy headband.

It's weird seeing her without the furry cosplay fox ears that usually rest on her head. Cheyenne is obsessed with Katsuki, her favourite anime character, and she likes to dress up as her. I'm used to it, but I always catch people giving her funny looks. Not that Cheyenne cares what anyone thinks. Sometimes I think she likes standing out because it makes everyone pay attention, as if she's daring them to say something about her fashion sense. I prefer going unnoticed.

Cheyenne's got Turner's syndrome, and she has to take special hormones to help her grow properly. Her mouth is plenty big though. I once watched her shut down a Year Eleven girl with just one sentence. The girl was chatting about my hair, so I guess she deserved it.

'Okay, where is it then?' Cheyenne's dark eyes scan the small room until she spots the swimming cap. 'Well, of course it won't fit,' she says. 'It's on the floor, you doughnut.'

Cheyenne is older than me, but she likes to act as if it's by years not months. She picks up the cap and her eyes widen in understanding. 'Rah, is your mum having a laugh?'

'I wish,' I reply. 'She thinks it's cute.' I flatten the *u* into an *oo* sound in imitation of Mum's strong Nigerian accent. Cheyenne smiles in instant recognition, her downturned eyes sparkling with glee.

I don't smile back. My eyes are fixed on the shiny swimming cap dangling from Cheyenne's middle finger. The bright white latex is covered in fire-engine-red spots.

Cheyenne's face is twitching, like she's trying to keep it straight. 'You know what you're gonna look like with all your hair crammed into that, don't ya?'

'Shut up,' I groan. Of course I know. It's all I've been thinking about today. I'm going to look like Toad from that classic Super Mario Bros game.

Her eyes shift to my head and the tangle of curls, coils and kinks sitting on top. It springs straight out of my head in an impressive riot that Mum finds overwhelming, so I rarely leave it loose. My hair has broken more combs, trashed more hairdryers and made more hairstylists cry than I can count ... so maybe Mum has a point.

Straightening it doesn't work, braids won't stay in for long and the only time Mum cut it, the strands grew back bigger and thicker. Now the longest bits that don't stick straight up or out, hang down my back almost to my bum. It always feels dry, no matter what I put in it, which doesn't help. The colour is cool though. A black so deep that when the light hits my hair just right, you can see bolts of blue fire shooting through it.

Cheyenne is proper laughing now. 'It's a-me, Mario!' she hollers with glee.

I wish I could laugh back, but I'm too stressed. It was

hard enough getting permission to even come swimming in the first place. Now that it's the school holidays, I'm either at Cheyenne's house or I have to stay at the salon so Mum can keep an eye on me. I left it until the last possible minute and waited until she was distracted with one of her clients before asking.

'Mum, can I leave early today please?' I asked.

Her hands stilled and silence descended on the salon. All conversation stopped as eager ears waited to hear Mum's reply.

'Why?' she finally said.

'Chey's having a pool party for her birthday,' I replied, not bothering to mention it was a party of two. At the sound of Cheyenne's name, Mum smiled, and I tried not to get my hopes up. 'Please, Mum,' I begged in a loud voice. 'You never let me go anywhere.'

'There you go again, always exaggerating,' Mum replied. 'Don't you go to school? Am I imagining your presence beside me at church on Sundays?'

I've learned not to answer questions like that. There *is* no right answer, so I remained silent.

'Why do you two want to go swimming anyway when Cheyenne gets all those ear infections?' she continued. 'You can't even swim very well.'

I ignored the bit about my rubbish swimming skills because she was right and I'd already told Cheyenne as much.

Mum was also right about the ear infections. Cheyenne gets them a lot because of the Turner's syndrome.

'It's been ages since Chey had one,' I replied instead. 'Besides, her mum said it was okay.'

Mum kissed her teeth at me. 'I do not want you out and about with so many strangers. You're not like everyone else.'

Not this again!

'Doesn't seem to bother you when I'm at the salon,' I muttered under my breath. 'There are always random people here!'

'What was that, Onyekachi?'

I plastered an innocent smile on my face. Mum is the only person who uses my full name and it's usually when I'm in trouble.

'Come on, Tópé, let the child have some fun,' Mrs Mataka said as she passed us on her way to the sink.

Hushed whispers spread across the salon and an annoyed look settled on Mum's face. She hates standing out almost as much as she hates me standing out. Then her face evened out suddenly, just before she gave in to the peer pressure she's always warning me about.

'Fine,' Mum finally said, and stunned relief filled me. I was fully ready for her to say no.

'But you must wear a swimming cap,' she added, and the relief melted away. 'I don't have time to wash and blow dry your hair today.'

Then Mum fully pulled out a swimming cap from one of her styling drawers. *Who has a swimming cap just hanging around?*

So here I am, trying to fit the ugly thing over my hair, and all Cheyenne can do is laugh. She finally stops spluttering long enough for me to get a word in.

'What am I going to do?' I ask.

'Sorry, fam, but you're gonna have to pack it up . . .'

My mouth twists and her voice trails off. Cheyenne meets my gaze again, but there's no curiosity or pity. Not like I get from others. To Cheyenne, my hair is just another part of me, like the gap between my front teeth and my massive size-eight feet. The same way I see her love of furry fox ears and marmite. It's the way I wish the world would see both of us, instead of only focusing on the things that make us different. It's what drew Cheyenne and me together in the first place.

That, and the fact she's the only other Nigerian I know. Mum never talks about Nigeria or why we left, so the little I know about how it became so rich and powerful comes from history class. It's been this way for as long as I can remember.

Before she found work in the salon, Mum cleaned toilets in one of the local primary schools. She was so thin then, her second-hand clothes hanging off her. She doesn't think I remember, but I do. I also remember how long it took for her to find a salon willing to ignore the fact she doesn't have a British passport and also willing to pay in cash.

'Everyone is going to be looking at me,' I tell Cheyenne with a sigh.

Cheyenne shrugs. 'Does it matter?'

She's right, it shouldn't. But it does to me.

I grab the swimming cap from her roughly and scrunch it up into a ball.

'Yes,' I reply.

Cheyenne hesitates for a moment, then pulls it from my clenched fist. 'I don't know why you let what other people think bother you so much,' she says, smoothing it out. She reaches towards me, the cap resting between her small fingers. 'We don't need to fit in.'

But I do, I want to scream. *I need to feel like I belong somewhere.*

I don't though. Instead, I push the frustration back down to join all the other feelings I'm not allowed to have, like curiosity about my father and happiness at school. And the scariest one of all . . . hope that things will be different.

'Look,' says Cheyenne after a short pause. 'It's my birthday and your mum finally let you do something other than go to church. I'm not letting you waste it by acting moist in here.'

My eyebrows lift at her tone, but she's right, and I don't want to mess up her special day. I snatch the ugly cap from her.

'You're the one who's moist,' I reply with a small smile.

'Sorry,' Cheyenne shoots right back. 'I can't hear you past your mushroom head.'

We quickly make our way poolside – a brightly lit, rectangular space that is even warmer than the changing room. The swimming cap tightens even more around my head.

In the middle of the space sits a large pool with people scattered everywhere. It's mostly kids, enjoying their summer holidays. Some are in the water, playing in lazy boredom, while the better swimmers zoom past them. The rest hang around the edge of the pool, chatting in small groups.

I feel the eyes and hear the sniggers following my bulbous head as we pass. A girl nudges past me with a wide-eyed look of wonder and I grit my teeth so I don't react. It's always the same and I've heard *all* the jokes. From how I look like a yeti to the *hilarious* one about using a rake to comb my hair.

Even adults, who should know better, can't help themselves. Every time we go to the hair shop to get products, Mum is always surrounded by people offering to do my hair, like it's so unbelievable that I would *choose* to walk around looking the way I do.

The worst part is watching Mum try to ignore them, her worry a constant blanket surrounding both of us. Mum says I shouldn't get angry or let it bother me when people chat rubbish. But when I see how sad it makes her and think about how she has to deal with it alone, I can't help but get angry. That's always when I wish my father was around. Mum says he felt things too deeply and his emotions would take over, just like mine. It's why he came up with the Fibonacci number sequence Mum then taught me – to stop his feelings overwhelming him.

Last year, Megan Gold said I tripped her on purpose. I didn't. The Velcro on her bag got caught in my hair. Ms Mason, our head teacher, didn't believe me and I got so upset I almost forgot to use my numbers. By the time I remembered, the prickles had spread from my scalp to my neck.

I wish my father were here so I could ask him how he dealt with his feelings. I'm sure Mum would be happier if he were here. I clutch the necklace round my neck. A single, white cowrie shell hanging from a thin, leather cord. It belonged to my father and it's the only physical connection I have to him.

Cheyenne coughs loudly, pulling me from my thoughts.

'Let's go,' she calls. 'My birthday only lasts for a day.'

I follow, silently. There are too many people and not

enough places to hide. Cheyenne and I usually just hang out in one of our bedrooms, watching our favourite anime. I love all the characters. In that world, being different is cool.

'There's a spot over there,' Cheyenne says, pointing to an empty space near the shallow end.

'Chey, I'm not sure about this,' I say, but she's already moving off and I rush to keep up.

'Ugh, will you just chill, Yeka,' she calls back, shortening my name, even though she knows I don't like it. 'You'll be fine once you get in.'

I catch up with her just as she reaches the edge of the water. 'But we're rubbish at swimming.'

'Shut up, I can totally swim,' Cheyenne says with a grin.

Cheyenne only just got her five-metre certificate. I know she's super proud and stuff, but I still don't understand why she thinks a pool party is a good idea.

Before I can say anything more, she steps into the pool and pushes forward until her body is fully submerged. *She makes it look so easy.*

I touch my head with nervous fingers and the stiff latex of the cap greets me. At least Mum will be happy. Then, with a deep breath, I follow Cheyenne into the pool.

The cold water is a shock, and my breath leaves my body in a sharp rush. How come no one else looks like they're swimming in a bowl of ice? I wade forward with gritted teeth until I'm waist deep in the water.

Cheyenne pulls an evil smile that proves she didn't warn me on purpose. The need for revenge takes over and, with a laugh, I splash towards her, giving her a shove.

Cheyenne stumbles backwards, surprised.

'I'm gonna get you for that,' she crows gleefully.

Before I know it, I'm fully underwater, Cheyenne's hands resting heavily on my shoulders. I struggle against her hold, pushing upwards until my head clears the surface.

Cheyenne gasps and her expression freezes. 'Rah, Yeka, I'm really sorry.'

Thick strands of hair now rest heavily on my shoulders, the ends swirling in the water around me. *So that's why the tight feeling around my head is missing.*

My chest pounds as heads turn in my direction while I search frantically for my swimming cap. By the time I spot it, it's well on its way to the deep end, weaving an impressive path between the thrashing bodies.

My eyes move back to Cheyenne's guilty-looking face, and I know she's seen it too. An uncomfortable silence stretches between us like a worn elastic band. Then something in Cheyenne's face changes and I see her eyes flick towards my cap.

'Chey, wait,' I call.

But I'm too late. Before I can stop her, Cheyenne turns, pushing towards it. Her body moves awkwardly through the water. But she can't keep up, and for every stroke she takes towards the cap, the swell of the moving water pushes it further away.

I want to yell at her to stop, to come back, but the thought of drawing more attention to myself freezes the words in my throat.

Then Cheyenne does stop, and a long shudder runs through her body. She starts flapping her arms frantically, as if she's in trouble. I swivel around to see if anyone else has noticed, but the world is still moving, totally oblivious. I turn back to Cheyenne in time to see her jerk once, before silently slipping under the water. The ripples go still. A second passes, then another, as my heart pounds a frantic rhythm in my chest.

Come on, Chey. Where are you?

Then something floats to the surface of the water. Something thin and red. Cheyenne's headband bobs up and down and I realize this is really happening.

'No, no, no,' I breathe out as panic snakes through me.

A part of me wants to run and hide, yet at the same time I know I need to call for a lifeguard. But fear has taken my voice. My gaze returns to Cheyenne's headband and my body makes the decision for me. I push forward, instinct taking over. My legs kick through the water in a clumsy rhythm, as if they have a mind of their own. *Maybe they do*. Maybe they somehow know that they need to get to Cheyenne.

When I reach the headband, I take a deep breath, then plunge downwards. Dark hair billows around me, dancing through the water, like swirling strings of blue-black ink. As my vision goes blurry, an eerie silence takes over and shafts of light stream into the water. I peer through it, searching for Cheyenne. I don't see anything at first, but then a dark blob at the bottom catches my eye.

I push downwards and wrap an arm around her small body before kicking out, trying to propel us upwards. But I'm too tired, and with the added weight of Cheyenne, it's even harder to move. My body seems to have finally remembered that I can't actually swim that well.

A prickle begins in my head, and my grip on Cheyenne loosens. We're going to die here, at the bottom of a swimming pool, in the middle of Woolwich. Panic fills my chest as prickling pain spreads through my body, and I try to calm down enough to think.

Zero . . . I count in my head.

I work to find a colour and texture, but all I can see is blue and all I feel is wet.

One . . . I try again, but I just can't hold onto it.

Anger courses through me. *I don't want to die. I don't want to leave Mum on her own!*

I kick out hard and try to swim to the surface, but my arms and legs aren't listening. My entire body is burning for oxygen. Then, suddenly, a sharp pain covers my entire scalp. The world around me transforms as my hair curves into a protective bubble, quickly surrounding us. My mouth opens, unable to believe my eyes, and water rushes in like a tidal wave.

Just as the water starts to slide down my throat, the bubble solidifies around Cheyenne and me, like a giant shield. For a moment, everything is still and strange and beautiful. Then, without warning, we start moving quickly towards the surface, pushed by the shield of hair. As my head clears the water, my hair melts away behind me like a dream, and an arm yanks us up. I gasp in some much-needed air, my chest heaving with the effort, and water streams from my eyes and nose as we are hauled to the side of the pool.

'Oh my God, what happened?'

Through my coughing and spluttering, the frantic voice of a lifeguard above me barely registers. I look over at Cheyenne.

'Chey?' I whisper.

She doesn't move.

'Chey!'

It's a scream this time, one that crawls from somewhere deep inside my belly. Heads turn in our direction, and a deafening silence falls as all activity seems to stop. Like hungry kids outside a chip shop, a crowd gathers around us. There are other lifeguards now, and I watch, numb with fear, as Cheyenne is swallowed by all the bodies. I lose sight of her and the pounding in my chest begins again, but there's also a new queasy tightness in my stomach. A steady beat and a rolling clench that combine into a painful rhythm.

'Are you okay?' I turn to find the lifeguard staring at me in a strange way. 'You all right?' he asks again.

I want to scream at the stupid question. 'Where are they taking her?' I ask instead, my voice hoarse.

He frowns, his eyes glued to my hair.

What's his deal?

'How did you manage to get her out?' he finally asks, ignoring my question.

There's a worrying note of suspicion in his voice, and I swallow hard. I don't know how to answer him because I don't know myself. One minute Cheyenne and I were done for, then suddenly there was all this hair.

My hair!

My stomach tightens and I reach up with a shaking hand. But it's just the usual thick strands. I look back down at the water. A thin, red headband bobs away, not too far from us, and next to it is a white and red swimming cap.

A lump settles in my throat. Cheyenne almost died ... and so did I. The thought is too horrible, too wrong, and I swallow again, trying to push saliva past the growing lump. I need to think about something else. My mind shifts back to the shield of hair that saved us. But it doesn't make any sense.

It couldn't have happened ... *could it?*

Tọlá Okogwu was born in Lagos, Nigeria, but raised in London, England. She holds a bachelor of arts degree in journalism. Having spent several years exploring the world of blogging, hair care and freelance writing, she finally returned to her first love: fiction. Tọlá is the author of the Onyeka fiction series, including the World Book Day novella, *Onyeka and the Secret Superhero*, the Daddy Do My Hair? picture book series, and the Aziza's Secret Fairy Door young fiction series under the pen name Lola Morayo. She now lives in Kent with her husband and two daughters.

Learn more at tolaokogwu.com.